E
WHI   WHITFIELD,PETER
        NO PRESENTS PLEASE

5/24 sc

6/26

ZEN TAILS™

NO PRESENTS PLEASE

WRITTEN BY PETER WHITFIELD

ILLUSTRATED BY NANCY BEVINGTON

SIMPLY READ BOOKS

"What a beautiful day!" Guru Walter Wombat declared as he sat in the shade of a large elm tree. "The sun is shining, the birds are singing and I do so love watching the trees swaying in the warm breeze!"

"What a rotten day!" grumbled Grizzel Bear as he stomped through the flowers. "The sun hurts my eyes, the birds screech and squawk, the trees are in my way, and the wind is messing up my fur!"

G rizzel Bear continued stomping until he happened to stomp right up to where Guru Walter Wombat was sitting quietly.

"What are you doing sitting in my stomping path?" Grizzel demanded.

Guru Walter just sat there. He smiled, he listened, but he said nothing.

"Get out of my way," Grizzel ordered furrowing his brow, "unless you want me to stomp on your head?"

Guru Walter Wombat just smiled.

"Why aren't you saying anything? Would you like me to give you a bone crunching Grizzel Bear squeeze?" Grizzel screamed, his temper rising.

Guru Walter Wombat just smiled.

"Didn't you hear me?" roared Grizzel even more loudly, shaking his large paw in Guru Walter Wombat's face. "Do you want a big punch on the nose?"

Guru Walter Wombat just smiled.

Grizzel was confused: Guru Walter Wombat didn't seem to react to him at all, and he was no longer full of stomping and screaming energy, but still feeling quite angry. "Haven't you got anything to say?" he demanded.

Guru Walter Wombat looked up at Grizzel Bear. "It is not my birthday," he said smiling back at him.

"What? Why are you telling me it's not your birthday?" Grizzel demanded. "I don't care about your birthday!"

"Then why are you trying to give me presents?" replied Guru Walter gently.

"What presents?" the confused Grizzel replied.

"**Y**ou tried to give me
a stomp on the head,

a bone crunching
Grizzel Bear squeeze

and a punch on
the nose.

I would not want those presents even if it were my birthday," said Guru Walter calmly. "I guess you will have to keep your anger all for yourself."

Grizzel glared at Guru Walter Wombat sitting amongst the grass and the flowers.

He growled at Guru Walter's still smiling face.

"I'm not angry!" he shouted, stomping on a daisy and crushing it into the ground.

"Really?" Guru Walter replied, raising an eyebrow, and pointing to the broken flower beneath Grizzel's foot.

Grizzel lifted his foot and picked up the daisy, which now lay crushed in his paw.

"I didn't do that…" Grizzel protested, "…did I?"

Guru Walter Wombat just sat, he smiled, but he said nothing.

Grizzel looked at the daisy and frowned. He was a big burly bear but he never really meant to hurt anyone or anything.

"I'm sorry little flower, I didn't mean to crush you. I was… I was …angry," Grizzel admitted. "I didn't see you. But I will try not to crush any more flowers today."

And true to his word, for the rest of the day, Grizzel Bear was very careful of all the flowers in the forest, and all the birds, and all the trees.

Zen

The Buddha was sitting in the shade of a tree when an
angry man came upon him. The angry man started yelling
insults, but the Buddha sat there calmly and said nothing.
The angry man continued screaming, but received no reply.
After about five minutes the man could not keep up his anger at
such a level and asked, "Do you have nothing to say?"
The Buddha asked the man, "If someone gives you a gift and you
do not want it, to whom does it belong?"
The man answered that it must remain with the giver of the gift.
Then the Buddha said, "I refuse to accept your anger, so you
will have to keep it yourself."
The angry man is said to have become a disciple
of the Buddha.

Tail

Grizzel had spent so much time being angry that he
had forgotten he was angry. You don't have to be angry just
because someone else is. It is much better to let go of anger
than to hold on to it, even if someone tries to give it to you.
Being happy is much more fun!

Published in 2006 by
Simply Read Books

www.simplyreadbooks.com

First published in Australia by New Frontier Publishing

10 9 8 7 6 5 4 3 2 1

Cataloguing in Publication Data
Whitfield, Peter, 1962-.
No Presents, please / Peter Whitfield ; illustrated
by Nancy Bevington

(Zen Tails)
ISBN 1-894965-23-X

I. Bevington, Nancy II. Title. III Series: Whitfield, Peter 1962- Zen tails.

PZ7. W53No 2006   j823'.92   C2005-900702-8

Designed by Nancy Bevington
Edited by Gabiann Marin & Christina Karaviotis
Printed in Hong Kong